REVENGE OF THE SIS

A Christina Starspeeder Story

Jarrett J. Krosoczka & Amy Ignatow

Scholastic Inc.

For River, Willow, and Nova.
—Jarrett

To Sara and Alex
Sure, you can go to Tosche Station to get some power
converters. Have fun!
—Amy

Scholastic Children's Books,
Euston House, 24 Eversholt Street,
London NW1 1DB, UK
A division of Scholastic Ltd

London ~ New York ~ Toronto ~ Sydney ~ Auckland
Mexico City ~ New Delhi ~ Hong Kong
First published in the US by Scholastic Inc, 2019
This edition published in the UK by Scholastic Ltd, 2019

A CIP catalogue record for this book is available from the British Library.

Printed by CPI Group (UK) Ltd, Croydon, CR0 4YY

Papers used by Scholastic Children's Books are made from wood grown in sustainable forests.

2 4 6 8 10 9 7 5 3 1

Heptaday

I'm giving up. Sleep is for other people. Besides, I'm pretty sure that Jedi Masters don't sleep. I spent three years at the Jedi Academy on Coruscant and I don't even think I ever saw Master Yoda sleep. When you're one with the Force, you don't need sleep because you're utterly calm with all the understanding of the universe flowing through you. Probably.

Jedha is going to be so different from Coruscant! I mean, I learned so much there but it kind of felt like practice. Jedha is the real deal. I'm going to be apprenticing with my very own Jedi Master. We'll be traveling to all sorts of different planets, and doing the real Jedi work of keeping peace and balance in the universe. No more practice! But I know I'm ready for anything. Or most things. I think I'm ready?

I really wish I had gotten more sleep.

8

I know you don't want to talk about it, and that's fine. But people are going to be curious about our dad. They're going to want to know why he became a Sith and put us all in danger.

Because he's a jerk-faced jerk.

I know. And you're nothing like him.

But . . . but we both love skyhopper races. And we're both strong with the Force . . .

Yup. But you have to remember that you're not a jerk-faced jerk.

Okay.

And I'm just a holocall away if you need to talk.

Thanks, big sis.

Monoday

I told Victor that he was going to be okay. He's a good kid. But I feel bad about leaving him so soon after he learned the awful truth about our father.

But he's going to be fine! Probably?

Get it together, Starspeeder, because in a few hours you're going to be meeting your new mentor, Skia Ro. Yes, THE Skia Ro. The very same Skia Ro who defeated Darth Kozyr in the Battle of Jabo, THE Skia Ro who survived for two years alone on the remote planet of Traal with only her wits and a towel, THE Skia Ro whose wise counsel brought lasting peace to Hosnian Prime, THE Skia Ro who designed the double-bladed lightsaber (not that anyone ever used one but still . . .) THE SKIA RO.

I can't believe that I get to have her as my Jedi Master! I mean, I can believe it, but it still gives me chills to think of everything I'll be learning from her. I need to calm down so she doesn't think I'm a jittery freak when we meet. Thinking calm thoughts. Feeling the Force flowing through me.

CALM THOUGHTS.

Blarfs, that didn't work. Might as well make sure I've packed everything.

Packing checklist:

Toothbrush
Toothpaste
Hair cones
Light robe (for warm tropical planets)
Snow robe (for cold ice planets)
Thermal underwear
Swimsuit (for hot swamp planets)
Lightsaber
Datapad
Datapad charger
Jedi Academy Award for Bravery
Space trip snacks
Blooey (small stuffed bantha)
Card from Victor

I feel like I'm forgetting something, but everyone always feels like they're forgetting something, right? Mr. Zefyr told us that everything we needed was already within ourselves, but I don't have a good pair of snow boots within myself. Did I pack my snow boots? What if I didn't and Skia Ro needs me to help her and I can't because of frozen toes?

CALM THOUGHTS!

TheRealSaraiAlx: Finally recording that solo album! #BoogieTime

👍 20K 💚 1M

GoongaTheHutt400: Come down to my racetracks and place your bets! #HuttCasino #Scarif

👍 2M 💚 1M

ProfessorAfos: New book out today! #Gastropods #GalacticZoology

👍 2K 💚 7K

GALAXY FEED

20 Things Maz
Kanata Wishes
She Knew When
She Was 400

Wookiee
Poverty on
the Rise

Surprising
Facts about
Bantha Poop

GALACTIC ZOOLOGY TODAY

Wampa, There It Is
By D'ian Afos

We've all heard tales of icy-breathed
adventurers meeting their gruesome
ends at the paws of Hoth's most
aggressive predator, the wampa. But new
zoological studies have shown that not
only are wampas vicious, they're also
exceptionally clever, with the patience
to set traps and wait for their prey to
come to them. It has also been discovered
that throwing scientific equipment at them
does not really serve to deter them from
their purpose, and really just face-to-
face with a wampa the best course of
action is to avoid its face. And claws.
Running away is ideal.

As carnivores, the main staple of the
wampa diet is whatever warm-blooded
creatures they can find, regardless of
whether or not they are native to
Hoth. Tauntauns make for good eating,
certainly . . .

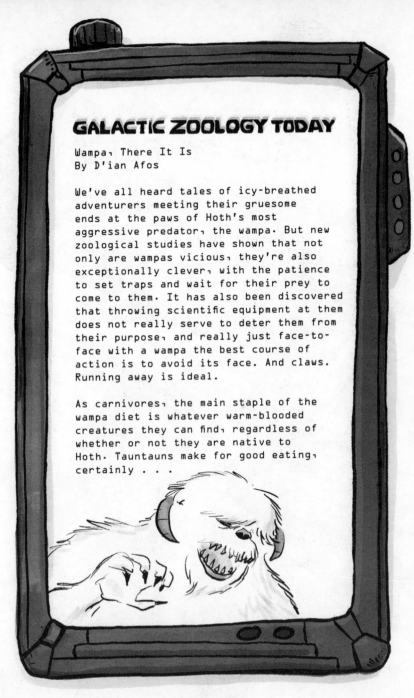

I'm Xel Chardin.

I'm Christina Starspeeder.

Are you new?

Yes, I just graduated from the Coruscant campus.

Never been there.

Yeah, I think I would have noticed you.

Why?

So which dorm are you in?

20

Everyone here is amazing.

Lyndar Syrush is basically already a legend for his popular Stargram.

Kyt Borksmit is a mechanical genius who invented her own transdimensional lightsaber.

Frk Khr Drn seems to know about every single planet in the galaxy.

How am I going to impress Skia Ro with apprentices like these everywhere I look?

Oh . . . okay! What ship? Is Skia Ro already on the ship? I'm so excited to finally meet her.

Of course you are.

Do you know where we'll be going first?

Yes.

So . . . where?

The ship.

Triday

Skia Ro's droid, Q-13, has put me to work loading up her ship, the *Faravahar*. Victor would freak out if he were here—the *Faravahar* is like no ship I've ever seen. I'm usually not into starships, but this is incredible!

Q-13 is definitely not like the droids on Coruscant. They were a lot more ... helpful. Maybe this is a lesson? Of course! I must learn to focus on the task at hand and prove that I'm willing to do what it takes to be a worthy apprentice, even if Skia Ro isn't around. Although she should be here any microsecond ...

The *Faravahar* is prepared for departure, Master Ro.

Very well. Chart a course for Kashyyyk.

Hello, Master Ro, I'm your new apprentice—

Young Starspeeder. You may proceed to the cockpit.

Am ... am I flying the *Faravahar*?

No.

Right, right, I figured I wouldn't, that would be a lot.

On my first day.

Quadday

Skia Ro is very . . . direct. Refreshingly direct! She just gives me the information that I need to know and not much else, which is fine, because who needs their minds cluttered up with extra details, right? Not me, I guess. She's definitely less approachable than Master Yoda.

Looks good on me, does it not?

We're heading to Kashyyyk, where some Wookiee clans have started fighting each other. I almost laughed when Master Ro told me about it, seeing how every Wookiee I've ever known has been like a great big fluffy snugglebunny. Back on Coruscant, Kitmum was basically just a really tall Ewok who taught me all the best phrases in Shyriiwook. But when I mentioned Kitmum to Q-13, they seemed to think that was an invitation to describe every horrific thing that Wookiees can do.

You should probably keep in mind that a Wookiee can . . .

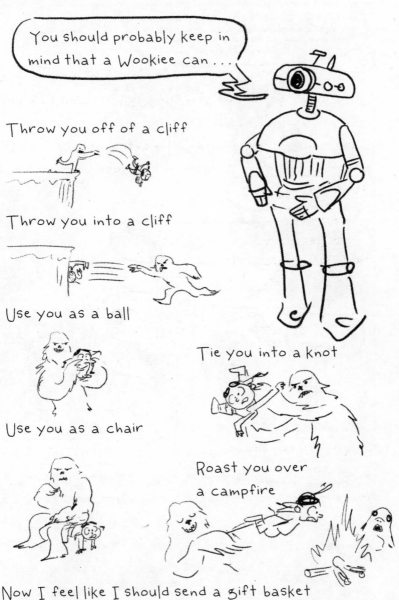

Throw you off of a cliff

Throw you into a cliff

Use you as a ball

Tie you into a knot

Use you as a chair

Roast you over a campfire

Now I feel like I should send a gift basket or something to Kitmum for never tossing me off a cliff.

You have seen a Wookiee before, yes?

Yes?

They look like that.

Awwwwooooorrrgggghh*

*translation: Hello, I am a root vegetable.

RAAWWWRRGGHH.

Rooooaarrrrrggguuurrrgh*

*translation: You have a tall face.

GWOOOORRKKKAARRR!

WAAAARRROOOOGGGHGH!

Arrooooooggghhh*

*translation: Behold the place of farts!

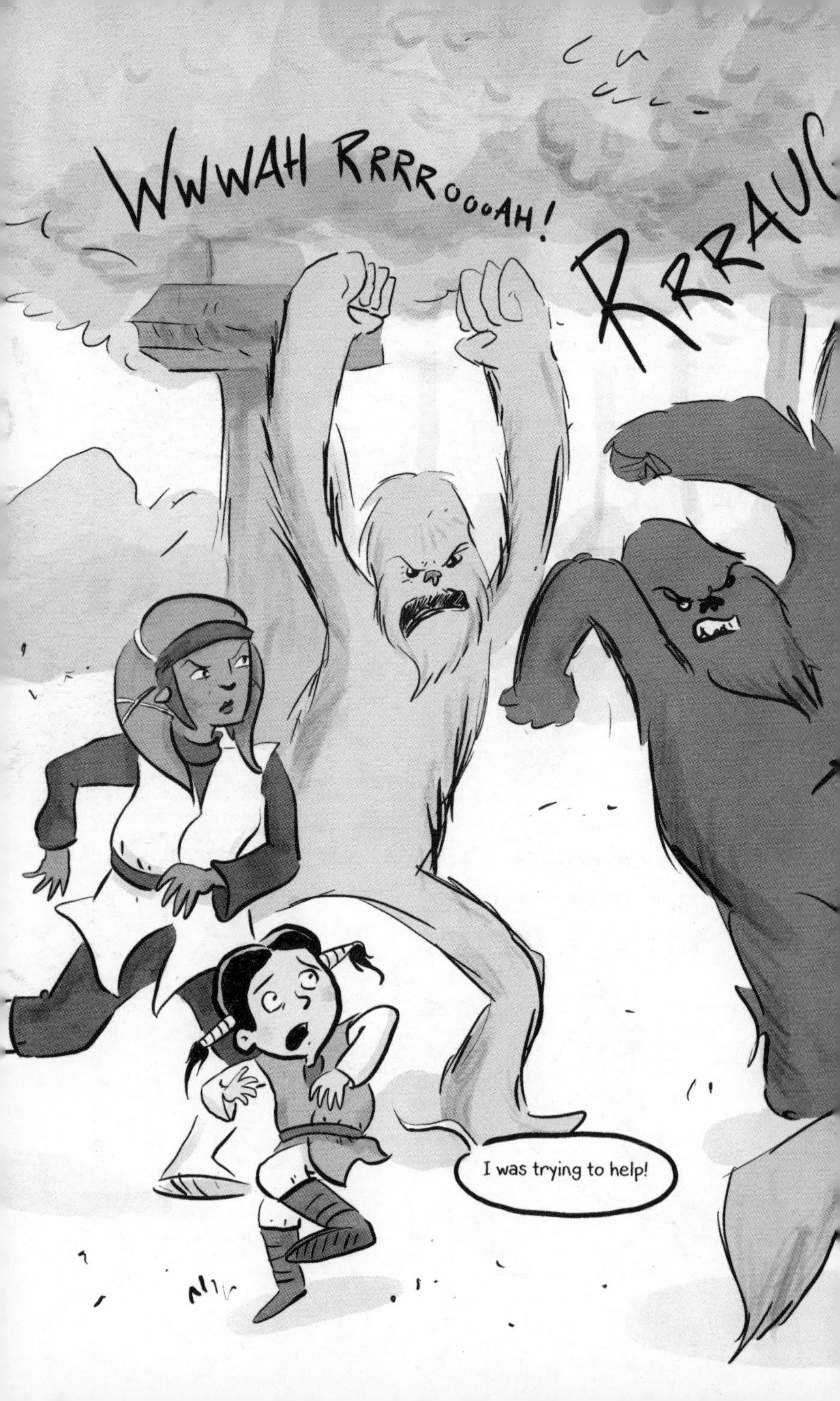
WWWAH RRRRROOOOAH!
RRRAUG
I was trying to help!

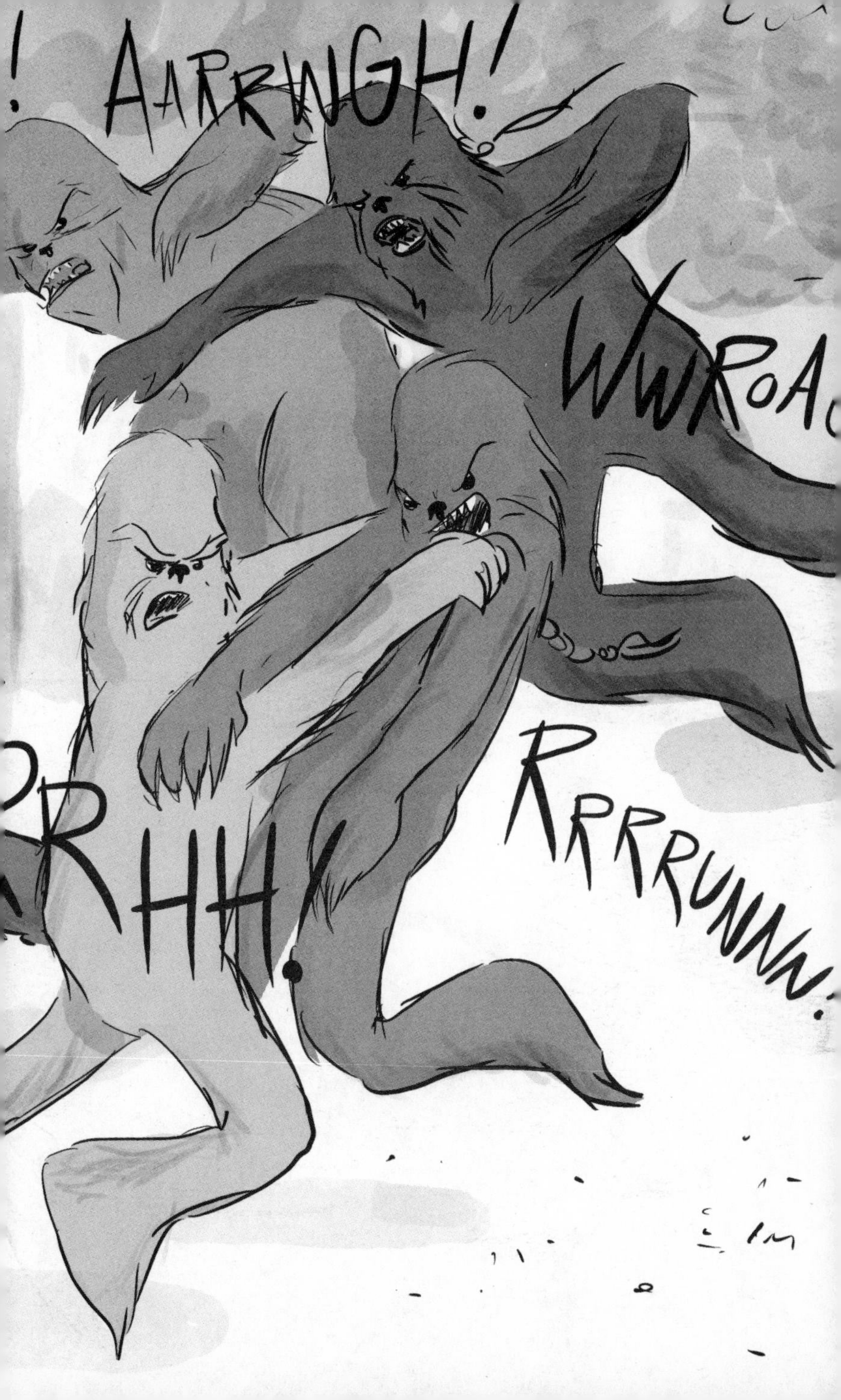
AARRWGH!
WWROA
RRHH!
RRRRUNNN!

JEDI MASTER BRINGS PEACE TO KASHYYYK

Skia Ro, in an act of fear-lessness that we've come to expect from the Jedi Master, has managed to calm tensions between two skirmishing Wookiee clans. Wookiee witnesses were very impressed with Master Ro's skills, not to mention her removal of a tree that had been suffering from a phosflea infestation.

"AAARROOOGGUUGGHH," said Hoorrakkik, echoing the sentiments of many local Wookiees, who all expressed gratitude and relief that the Grrobahrr and Chevappa clans are once more staunch allies.

According to the Wookiees on the scene, the growing feud had been exacerbated by the arrival of Master Ro's new apprentice, who managed to make things worse by threatening them with her own flatulence. Skia Ro has denied that controlled farting is a new Jedi skill.

GALACTIC ZOOLOGY TODAY

Nexu: The Lightweight Ravenous Beast We'd
All Like to Avoid
By D'ian Afos

One of the first lessons a zoologist must
learn is that death is a part of life;
what is born will eventually die, whether
it is a mysterious Barri existing for
thousands of years on the tail of a comet
or a Felucian ground beetle that lives for
less than a standard week. All lives must
end. But if you can avoid a confrontation
with a murderous nexu, your end may not
be extremely terrible.

Lightweight and agile, nexu use their
infrared vision to track their prey, which
they are able to easily tear limb from
limb with their incredibly sharp teeth
and razor-like claws. Because of their
light build the nexu are able to leap up
to four times their own height, which
means that painful death often comes from
above for their victims. Unlike a heavier
predator, however, a nexu can be felled
with a well-placed blow . . .

Pentaday

We're headed back to Jehda and Master Ro hasn't said one word about my massive fail on Kashyyyk. She's hardly said one word about ... anything. This is not the case with Q-13.

Oh, but you're the Wookiee expert who can speak fluent Shyriiwook.

Weird how you never noticed that most Wookiees can understand Galactic Basic.

Q-13 is easily the most obnoxious droid I've ever met. But the worst part is that he's not wrong—how could I have been such a gundark brain? It's like I threw all of Master Yoda and Mr. Zefyr's training into a garbage compactor. I need to pull myself together for the first day of mission reports.

We learn from observation and experience—both our own and those of our fellow apprentices.

Congratulations on surviving your first missions! Let's talk about what we saw and heard and felt and smelled.

And then Master Ojiee stopped the charging Trandoshans by suggesting they take deep breaths!

Master Cor never even took out her lightsaber!

I don't know how he did it, but it took something like two nanoseconds for Master Sammeh to get those Ewoks to stop rioting and start dancing.

Master Mun won't let me take her picture . . .

And you, young Starspeeder? What did you experience?

Duoday

Is there a word for "beyond embarrassing"? Maybe "MEGAEMBARRASSING." Or maybe I already said the word for "beyond embarrassing" only I said it in Shyriiwook and had no idea what I was saying.

I just know everyone read that article about what happened to us on Kashyyyk; they're just being too polite to say anything about it.

Why is this so hard? Coruscant wasn't exactly easy but I always knew what I was doing, and everyone else knew I could do it! But now I feel like the only one expecting anything is Q-13 and they're expecting me to be a massive failure. I'm pretty sure I'm meeting expectations.

A⁺ failure Starspeeder!

I wish Victor were here. It would be nice to have someone to talk to. Also, he'd probably do something a thousand times worse than what I did and then maybe I wouldn't look like such a dum-dum womp rat.

GALAXY FEED

A Buyers' Guide to Protocol Droids

Scavenging! Not Just for Jawas.

Reforms at Coruscant Jedi Academy. Are They Worth It?

THE DAILY MILLENNIUM

New Allegations of Musical Piracy Fuel Clashes among Bith on Clak'dor VII

The Bith music world has been rocked by a stunning accusation of plagiarism. Accomplished kloo hornist and known heartthrob Or'bin Gella has been accused of stealing his most beloved composition, *The Turtleneck Boogie*, from his former bandmate, Sarai Alx. The rumors and subsequent promises of retribution have shaken the Bith population.

"I don't know how this could happen," Alx was overheard by anonymous witnesses while sobbing over her gasan string drum, "but I feel like the only recourse is to gather my loyal fanbase and urge them to attack his loyal fanbase."

"*TURTLENECK BOOGIE* WAS STOLEN!" Doon Mup, a frustrated young music student at the Royal Clak'dor VII Conservatory was overheard wailing as he used his fanfar to bludgeon a fellow Bith who happened to be wearing a limited edition Or'bin Gella vest. He was soon apprehended but tensions remain high.

Hexaday

Everyone is talking about what's been happening on Clak'dor VII (which is kind of nice because when they're talking about that I know they're not talking about me). Still, it's awful. And the Bith are so gentle! Back on Naboo, my Bith fanfar instructor was the sweetest, most patient teacher I've ever had. Her people have gone thousands of years without any fighting—why are they starting now?

To the ship.

Right.

So, would it kill you to tell me where we're actually going? Like, in the ship?

No.

No, you're not going to tell me?

No, it would not kill me.

Come on. Is it another peacekeeping mission?

Every Jedi mission is ultimately a peacekeeping mission.

You're the worst.

We're going to Clak'dor VII.

Wow, you were right, that didn't actually kill you!

I'm always right.

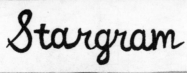

Stargram

SpeedyC: I think @FrkForce720 has fallen in love. #BanthaFluff

XelThaKiffar: What even is this. #Breakfast #Jedha #Why

Number1Lyndar: Me and the hem of Master Mun's robes! #WillGetThatPhoto #OnlyAMatterOfTime

Faarkoba1113: Ooooraaaaaww ggrooooowwooorr!
#Ooooooorrrgggrrr

BeepBoopBorksmit: New pocket taloscope!
#Gadgets #Bliss

ProfessorAfos: Abandoned exogorth tunnel!
#StillSmells

Monoday

Clak'dor VII is a pretty long trip from Jedha, or maybe it just seems like a long trip because neither Q-13 nor Master Ro is talking to me. I used to be so annoyed with the trips from Naboo to Coruscant because Victor would just always be all...

...the entire way there, but it was better than this silence. I kind of want to put on some music in the name of "research," but Master Ro doesn't seem like she'd be into Bith music. Or any music. Or any noise. Particularly from me.

I wish we were talking about the mission, though, because it's strange to think of Bith getting into fights. I mean, it was also super odd that the Wookiees were fighting each other. Who's next? Are we going to be seeing some droid-on-droid violence?

It's such a small thing. Yet give it to the right person, and it can bring joy to millions.

I fear my people are no longer capable of joy.

Perhaps.

But we never know what we're capable of until we try.

Yes! Music is the key. Music will bring everyone together.

Triday

What I thought would happen . . .

This music touches our hearts and we feel reconnected with our essential peaceful nature, hooray!

CRASH!

CRASH!

Behold, my Bith friends! The noises have stopped. But please stay. Or'bin Gella has agreed to play again. Music will bring us all together.

As soon as my tone-deaf apprentice gets these instruments repaired.

GO.

After consulting with Q-13 (who somehow proved that a droid can smirk) I was able to find an instrument repair shop. I had no idea how I was going to pay for the repairs, but once the owner heard I was Skia Ro's apprentice she waived her fee. Because, of course, everyone loves Skia Ro.

It's wonderful because it means that the Bith go with everything they read on their Stargrams and in The Daily Millennium.

Why wouldn't they?

Indeed, why wouldn't they? We should all immediately believe everything we read without checking other sources or listening to our own common sense.

AH HA HA HA HA HA HA!

What are you even talking about?

Why would anyone lie about this stuff? Who would want to make peaceful races fight?

60

That nasty Toydarian was probably just messing with me, right? Right?

Quadday

After I got the repaired instruments back to the cantina the band started up and all the Bith began to dance. It was amazing! I even saw Skia Ro do a few moves.

The music was incredible (Xel is going to be bummed he missed it) but I didn't dance. First, because I totally don't deserve to dance, and second, because I'm pretty sure that somehow my dancing would make everyone angry again.

THIS IS HORRIBLE! MAKE HER STOP! USE THE FORCE!

Also I couldn't stop thinking about what the Toydarian had told me. Was someone really trying to trick us? No, that's crazy. But what if it was true?

Heading back to Jehda now. This is going to be another fun ride.

64

Why are all the most peaceful races in the universe going bonkers?

THE DAILY MILLENNIUM

New Skyhopper Racetracks Being Built with Alarming Speed

Confirming rumors that have been swirling for several standard months, Goonga the Hutt announced today that he would be opening several new Skyhopper racetracks throughout the galaxy. So far racetrack construction has already begun on Ithor, Clak'dor VII, and Kashyyyk.

"Come down, place your bets. There is no better place to try your luck," the developer told reporters. When asked about any local resistance to the construction due to environmental concerns, Hutt was dismissive. "I think having the best tourist attraction in this star system makes up for a little dust, don't you?"

I felt as though people needed help. They were crying out for it.

I can see how that would be unnerving.

But I don't know if I can help anyone. I certainly haven't been helping Master Ro.

Sometimes we are able to help. And sometimes we cannot.

That wasn't very helpful.

See?

Duoday

Even though I still didn't know what to make of the voices I'd heard during meditation, I did feel a little better after talking with Master Poof (although just a little). I got the sense that he understood and knew what I had to do, but that he wants me to figure it out for myself.

Lessons on Coruscant were so much easier when there were clear answers to every question!

Speaking of ... Professor D'ian Afos from *Galactic Zoology Today* is coming to Jedha to give a lecture! When I saw the flyer I was so excited, and I don't even care that I'm the only one.

Take, for instance, the vicious reek of the planet Ylesia. Here we have an animal that is bred to kill. We know them be incredibly dangerous, particularly when they use their sharp central horn to impale their opponents.

But their true nature is quite gentle! Reeks are natural herbivores. Of course we've come to think of them as bloodthirsty killers, but that's only because the ones in captivity that have been trained to kill have been given a diet of meat.

This goes against everything we know to be right with the Force—only when we study and understand the true nature of every creature will we know how to use the Force to help and not harm them. Harming is easy. Helping takes work and study.

Hexaday

D'ian Afos was incredible. All the creatures she talked about were fascinating—who knew that Fyrnocks can't walk in sunlight? Not this apprentice! Or that the farts of dweebits are what make the entire planet of Belkadan uninhabitable? Amazing! Also, super disgusting. But still amazing!

But what really got me was how she talked about her study of the animals—how even the weirdest, grossest, most dangerous mess of a creature still has its place in the universe and how when we just believe the worst things about them, we'll never find out why they're important.

I can't believe I was the only one from my dorm to go to the lecture. I mean what could be better than learning about K'lor slugs? I know I'm not doing so great in the field with Skia Ro (okay, I'm doing TERRIBLY in the field with Skia Ro) but at least I'm trying to get everything I can out of being here.

Or maybe I'm the weird one. Am I the weird one?

Stargram

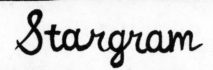

XelThaKiffar: Relaxin' with @FrkForce720 in the common room #HolographicChess #AlwaysWinning

FrkForce720: Poor @XelThaKiffar got his players all squished #FrownyFace #SoreLoser

SpeedyC: THE @ProfessorAfos signed my book! #SoExcited #Gastropods

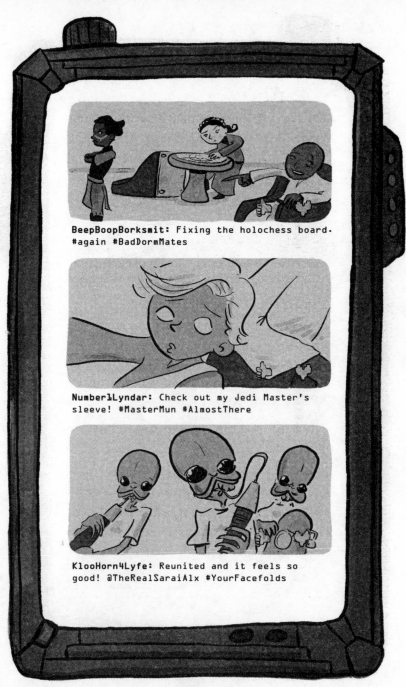

BeepBoopBorksmit: Fixing the holochess board. #again #BadDormMates

Number1Lyndar: Check out my Jedi Master's sleeve! #MasterMun #AlmostThere

KlooHorn4Lyfe: Reunited and it feels so good! @TheRealSaraiAlx #YourFacefolds

GALAXY FEED

See Tatooine
from the Back
of a Bantha

Surprising
Facts about
Maramu Poop

Skyhopper
Racers in
Desperate Need
of Beautiful
New Venues
Sponsored Post

GALACTIC ZOOLOGY TODAY

Porgs: Most Adorable Pet Ever or Dinner?
By D'ian Afos

No one can be blamed for never having
heard of Ahch-To, a planet in one of
the most remote and uninhabited corners
of our universe. But for those who are
willing to make the journey, the difficult
to reach rocky islands of Ahch-To reveal
a world of cuteness, for they are the
home of the porgs.

Wide-eyed and delightfully tubby,
these avians roost in the crags of the
cliffs overlooking the ocean, giving
them beautiful sunset views as well as
a good place to be on the lookout for
passing tasty fish. They are also fond
of crustaceans but are not discerning
eaters; porgs will attempt to eat pretty
much anything that they can stuff into
their beakless faces (including the
brand-new datapads of junior zoologists
who were careless enough to leave them
unattended). As they have no natural
predators on Ahch-To, porgs are very
friendly, which makes them exceedingly
easy to catch if you're in need of
protein . . .

Did you already mock her for her in-depth study of the fearsome . . .

. . . what even is a porg?

Yup, we covered that.

Did you ask her why she's even bothering to be a Jedi apprentice when it's clear she'd probably be better at being a zoologist?

No, that seemed overly harsh.

Give me that. I don't want to be a zoologist.

Then why are you wasting your time going to zoology lectures and reading long articles about fat little birds in remote corners of the galaxy where probably no Jedi will ever set foot?

Heptaday

Maybe Xel has a point. I mean, I wouldn't mind being a zoologist—I could travel all over the universe and go to all sorts of different planets and study creatures and be like D'ian Afos. That would be amazing! Plus I wouldn't have to worry about causing intergalactic mayhem or disappointing Master Ro again. I bet she'd welcome the news of my withdrawal from the program.

And as a native Naboo you will not be accustomed to Hoth's climate, so pack accordingly.

Yes, Master Ro.

Our mission is to rescue the family before they freeze to death or are eaten by hostile predators. This should be a fairly routine mission.

Yes, Master Ro.

So, please, young Starspeeder, just watch and learn. I understand your desire to participate, and someday you will. But even the most powerful Jedi knows that there are times when there's more to be learned from observation than from throwing oneself into the fray.

Yes, Master Ro.

Duoday

Having Master Ro talk directly to me without Q-13 around was nerve-wracking. But also kind of exciting! But mostly nerve-wracking. I was this close to telling her that I was thinking about quitting my training to become a zoologist, but she kind of doesn't invite a whole lot of back-and-forth conversation.

Chris, I need your help.

Just got a holocall from Victor, but I was getting on my Hoth gear (so many layers!) and didn't really have time to talk. He did not sound great—Mr. Zephyr has been fired? What on Coruscant is that all about? I feel I should be more worried but ... I don't know, I kind of trust the kid. I can't even believe I'm writing that, but I do. The Force is strong with him. I know he'll be all right.

See that pack of wild tauntauns over there?

Wow, I've read about them in *Galactic Zoology Today*!

Good. We're going to saddle up the two closest ones.

We're going to what now . . .

Follow my lead, do as I do, and don't be nervous. The tauntauns can sense fear.

Don't they smell wonderful?

Uh . . .

I am joking. That was a joke. They smell horrible. You'll get used to it.

This doesn't look good.

VWOOSH! VWOOOSH! VWOOOSH!

Quadday

The good news is that I think Master Ro and Q-13 have a newfound respect for me, which is really nice. For the first time in a long time I feel like maybe coming to Jehda wasn't a completely terrible idea. The bad news is that it is getting colder (HOW IS THIS EVEN POSSIBLE) so we're either going to freeze to death or be eaten by wampas.

Master Ro has sent me to the crashed ship to see if they have any supplies worth scavenging, but it's mostly just a junked shell—I can't imagine anyone actually flying it. I wish Victor were here to tell me what kind of a ship it is, because I don't recognize anything about it.

You're lookin' at a Z-Winged Fighter 4000, third generation.

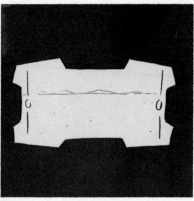

Time to go.

But I'm not finished!

Then finish.

Pentaday

I am grateful for three things: first, that Master Ro, Q-13, and I managed to work together to survive the trip to Hoth! Second, for nice warm baths. And third, for the fact that no one has commented on the fact that I yelled "Wampas are coming to wamp us." I blame the extreme cold.

GALACTIC ZOOLOGY TODAY

Gamorreans: Ladies First
By D'ian Afos

Long recognized as the universe's warrior-pigs-for-hire, the most fundamental aspect about Gamorrean culture is also the least known: Gamorreans have a matriarchy. While it is true that the males, or boars, are known as violent fighters, it is the females, or sows, that decide a boar's place in Gamorrean society.

The boars are recognized for their strength and ability to provide for their wives, and a sow will not choose to wed and promote a boar that does not measure up. Each Gamorrean clan is ruled by a Clan Matron that has the power to choose the male to lead beside her (known as a Warlord). So the easiest way to topple a Warlord is to shame him in front of his wife, who ultimately decides whether or not he is worthy of leadership.

Stout, with green, hairless skin, Gamorreans are easily recognized by their snouts and the protruding underbite of tusks . . .

THE DAILY MILLENNIUM

New Casino at Canto Bight!

In exciting news for the gambling world, Goonga the Hutt has announced the opening of his new casino and racetrack on Canto Bight. "This casino is going to be the ultimate playground in the universe," Hutt told reporters. "I suggest we use it to have some fun."

When asked about how he attained the nearly impossible-to-get permits required to open his new business on Canto Bight, Hutt was vague. "You know what they say about Hutts — we're fearless and inventive. Besides, if I gave away my secrets, where would the fun be in that?"

Despite concerns over the unusually fast pace of construction, Hutt Palace is scheduled to open on time to the public in one standard week.

Triday

When I saw that photo of Goonga the Hutt I felt uneasy, like I was seeing something familiar (in a bad way). And that's when I noticed the insignia that Hutt's bodyguards were wearing.

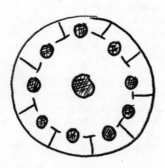

It was the same one from the downed ship on Hoth! Could it be that was an old starship of Goonga the Hutt's? What was it doing abandoned on Hoth and why were we called to "rescue" it?

Why are there all of a sudden so many stories going around about violent Wookiees, cheating Bith, and fighting Ithorians?

And why is it that there are fights breaking out on every peaceful planet where Hutt is setting up one of his skyhopper racetracks?

This all seems like too much coincidence. What did Mr. Zephyr once say?

If it looks like a nexu, and drools like a nexu, and smells like a nexu, it's probably a nexu and you should start running because it wants to murder you.

I have to tell Master Ro!

Calm down, both of you. Young Starspeeder, say your piece.

I . . . okay . . . Goonga the Hutt's bodyguards were wearing the same insignia that I saw on the abandoned starship on Hoth. And there has been crazy fighting on every usually peaceful planet where he's been building skyhopper tracks. I think he's behind the fighting and also the reason that we were sent to Hoth to get eaten by wampas!

These are serious accusations, Christina.

I know. And it all sounds kind of crazy now that I've said it out loud.

Perhaps you should have thought more before you did. I shall meditate on all you have said. You are dismissed.

A distraction from what?

I think that Goonga the Hutt is trying to distract everyone from the fact that he's building cheap, noisy, polluting Skyhopper racetracks right next to where they live. And I think he tried to get rid of Master Ro for stopping the fights.

Whoa.

Goonga the Hutt?

You really do want to get kicked out.

Go ahead. Say I should become a zoologist.

I think you're onto something.

Pentaday

Xel and I talked for a long time. He told me that his family once owned a really nice beachfront hotel on Scarif. It was small but popular, and the only hotel on the little island until Goonga the Hutt came and began building another, bigger hotel. Xel's family couldn't do anything to stop it, and Hutt's promises of getting paid a metric ton of money convinced most of their employees to leave and work for him. It wasn't very long before their little family-owned hotel went out of business and they were forced to move back to the Kiffar homeworld of Kiffu.

What really stung is that there were plenty of undeveloped islands on Scarif where Hutt could have built a hotel—he just chose ours because we'd already done so well there.

It took only a few months for us to close our hotel.

We still get holomail from our old employees telling us that he treats them badly.

A Message from the Jedi High Council

The Padawans of Jedha have been invited to join their masters to supply additional security at the opening of Hutt Casino in the city of Canto Bight on Cantonica. As it is your first assignment together we expect you to use what you have learned with your Masters and apply it to work as a team. This is a prestigious assignment and we look forward to a peaceful event.

Why are we even doing this? Guarding a new casino does not seem like the best use of the Force.

They know that Goonga the Hutt is a nightmare, right? They can't actually believe that he's someone they can reason with. Can they?

Would you guys quit doubting our Masters? You're going to get the rest of us in trouble.

We should check out the place.

Maybe we can find some proof of your theory.

Or we could just stay put and not get into trouble.

And where do you think you're going?

We are the apprentices of Jedi Masters Ojiee, Ro, Mun, Sammeh, and Cor.

And I care . . . why?

We were invited to be here!

To work, you filthy little baby Jedi, not to get your grubby paws all over everything.

They're ruder than you.

Just sit down and wait for the Masters to come back.

Heptaday

This is getting ridiculous. We have been sitting here FOREVER. Frk has been meditating so long she may have actually become one with the Force. Or she's sleeping. It's hard to tell because she doesn't have eyelids. Lyndar's taken over 78 holophoto selfies, and out of sheer boredom Kyt has disassembled her pocket taloscope to make a teeny, tiny dancing droid. Q-13, predictably, is no help. I can't tell if the Masters are refusing to tell us anything because that's how they always are or if they're refusing to tell us anything because they genuinely don't know anything.

Stop whining. They'll be back soon.

Wow. Lyndar wasn't kidding about the toilets.

Are you serious?

I'm telling you! I hear that Goonga is looking for new dancers and entertainers for his casino.

Ugh, gross.

I'm going to audition. He's going to take over the whole galaxy soon. We might as well get on his good side.

He's not going to take over anything. The Jedi would never allow it.

We need to find the Masters.

You're bored and letting your imaginations get the best of you.

Sit. Down.

Look, Q-thir, I get that you can't feel the Force, but you know it's not like the Masters to just leave us here for so long without checking in.

Doesn't that tell you that something isn't right?

We have to follow their instructions . . .

No, I'll post this photo to Lyndar Syrush's Stargram with a hashtag of "GamorreansHurtKids" and wait for your wives to see you beating up CHILDREN.

That's right. You're Gamorrean, and Gamorreans are a matriarchal society. That means that when your Clan Matron sees you hurting kids she's going to kick you out of the clan. You'll lose your wives, your statuses, EVERYTHING. All I have to do is press this button. But I won't as long as you PUT. HER. DOWN.

I need to start reading *Galactic Zoology Today*.

We ran (and ran and ran some more) until we found an empty fathier stable where we could catch our breaths and come up with a plan to find the Masters.

I am Q...14, and I'm here to meet the boss.

I don't think so.

My presence was requested by Goonga the Hutt himself.

HA!

147

beep
boop
?

Master Cor
is out!

I cannot
see...

beep
boop

BOOF

Hello, Master Ro!

Get them before they regain their sight!

I don't need my sight to know where you are, Hutt.

GAAHHH!

Did I get him?

Um, no.

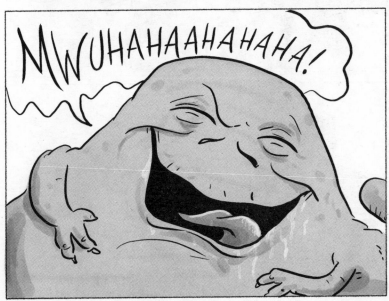

MWUHAHAAHAHAHA!

THE DAILY MILLENNIUM

A stunning close-quartered battle between the hired Gamorrean Guards of mogul Goonga the Hutt and a group of Jedi Masters and their apprentices came to an abrupt halt last night when Hutt began to choke on some Ahch-Tovian delicacies. Because of his large size it took all nine of his associates as well as several Jedi to stop him from choking and dislodge the vittles.

Once the danger of Hutt's choking to death had passed and the Gamorreans had been subdued by the Jedi, the cause of the fight was revealed: according to records, associates of Goonga the Hutt have been planting stories on Stargrams and in periodicals in order to cause dissention among several normally peaceful species. Distracted by rumors that led to violent skirmishes, Wookiees on Kashyyyk, Bith on Clak'dor VII, and other races have neglected to notice that their lands were being used to build shoddily constructed Skyhopper tracks. "Had we realized what was happening we never would have allowed it," Premier Brak Werpung of Clak'dor VII said, surveying the crumbling, leaking structure on her planet. "AROOOOOWWRRRR," echoed Phradyyr of Kashyyyk.

"Get your hands off me!" Goonga the Hutt was reported to shout as the Jedi Masters led him away to be questioned. "Don't you know who I am? Do you have any idea? I'm Goonga the Hutt!"

In related news, authorities in Canto Bight have announced that Hutt's new casino, Hutt Palace, will be shuttered due to major health code violations regarding toxic aurodium-colored paint on the toilets.

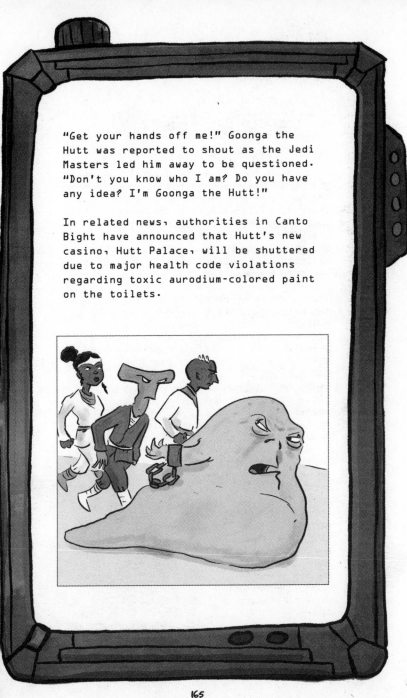

Heptaday

It feels a strange to be back on Jedha. Everything feels a little different. I'm much less intimidated by the Jedi Masters now that I know even they can be captured and then stumble and bump into each other. Even they need help sometimes, and when my friend s and I work together, we can be the ones to help them! It's kind of nice to know.

But it's also a little scary. My whole life I've just assumed that a Jedi Master can do pretty much anything, and I wanted to be just like that. Now I see they put on their robes one arm at a time like the rest of us.

Xel and the others also say they feel more comfortable around their Masters. We're all definitely a lot more comfortable around Q-thir.

167

You did have some . . . stumbles.

I don't know why it took me so long to get my footing. I always did so well on Coruscant.

I have learned that the flow of the Force favors those who use it to help, rather than to impress.

So you're saying I was probably working a little too hard to make you like me.

Perhaps it would be best if you never again attempt to play the fanfar.

Hexaday

I can't believe I'm already going back to Coruscant to watch Victor graduate! On one hand, it feels like I just got to Jehda—on the other, I could swear I've been here for at least a thousand years and saying good-bye is harder than I'd imagined.

Come visit me on Kuat!

Catch me on Stargram!

I'm going to miss you!

May the Force be with you.

Q-13, I got you a little something.

Okay.

Christina?

Yes?

Don't let the wampas wamp you.

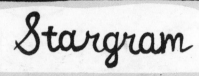

SpeedyC: Look at my baby brother go!
@VICT-orious #JediAcademyCoruscant #Graduation

👍 6 💚 28

VICT-orious: Okay, I admit it, I missed
@SpeedyC #BestSister

👍 4 💚 9

BeepBoopBorksmit: Building a lil' droid!
#DroidLife

👍 4 💚 7

Jarrett J. Krosoczka is a *New York Times* bestselling author, a two-time winner of the Children's Choice Book Award for the Third to Fourth Grade Book of the Year, an Eisner award nominee, and is the author and/or illustrator of more than thirty books for young readers. His work includes several picture books, the Lunch Lady graphic novels, and Platypus Police Squad middle-grade novel series. Jarrett has given two TED Talks, both of which have been curated to the main page of TED.com and have collectively accrued more than two million views online. He is also the host of The Book Report with JJK on SiriusXM's Kids Place Live, a weekly segment celebrating books, authors, and reading. His graphic memoir, *Hey, Kiddo*, was a National Book Award Finalist.

Jarrett lives in western Massachusetts with his wife and children, and their pugs, Ralph and Frank.

Amy Ignatow is the author and illustrator of The Popularity Papers series and the Odds series. She lives in Philadelphia with her family and really, really wants a lightsaber.